Padma Shri Pran

Maurice Horn, the editor of World Encyclopedia of Comics, has described cartoonist PRAN as Walt Disney of India.

Entertaining generation after generation, his comics have been constant companion of all the growing youngsters providing fun and amusement through his famous characters like CHACHA CHAUDHARY, SABU, SHRIMATIJI, PINKI, BILLOO, RAMAN etc. More than 600 of his titles are selling well in the market, and numerous comic strips are regularly appearing in various newspapers. His CHACHA CHAUDHARY comics had already been adapted for a TV Serial, and ran continuously for 600 episodes on a premier channel.

Travelling widely over the globe, he delivers lectures at various International Conferences. He has also been honoured with 'People of The Year Award' by Limca Book of Records for popularizing comics. His comic book 'United We Stand' was released in 1983 by the then Prime Minister Mrs. Indira Gandhi, and is still very popular among children.

Publisher

BUT THEY ARE CRUSHING INNOCENT PEOPLE UNDER THEIR TANKS...

EVEN THIS ISN'T ENOUGH. AT TIMES THEY GET BOMBS DROPPED ON THEM THROUGH JET PLANES. THOSE WHO SURVIVE, CROSS THE BORDER AND COME TO OUR NATION.

SUGGEST ANY ONE NAME WHO CAN GO TO THEIR PRESIDENT.

CHACHA CHAUDHARY !
© PRAN'S FEATURES

PRIME MINISTER OFFICE'S CAR?
THEY MUST HAVE BROUGHT AN OFFER FOR YOUR IDLE CHACHA TO JOIN POLITICS.
CHACHAJI! THE GOVERNMENT WANTS TO SEND YOU TO THE NEIGHBORING COUNTRY AS ITS REPRESENTATIVE.
REST WE CAN DISCUSS ON THE WAY.
WHY IS DICTATOR ROTANDA KILLING HIS OWN CITIZENS?
HE FEELS THAT THE OTHER GROUP WANTS TO OVERPOWER HIM.
TAILORS
GENTS' SUITS
SHOES
STUDIO

ROTANDA.
YOUR EXCELLENCY! CHACHA CHAUDHARY, THE REPRESENTATIVE OF INDIA WANTS TO TALK TO YOU.
HELLO SIR!

SO YOU ARE SAYING THAT OUR INNUMERABLE CITIZENS HAVE COME TO YOUR COUNTRY AND GIVEN RISE TO LAND AND FOOD PROBLEM? WHY DON'T YOU KILL THEM? PROBLEM SOLVED!!

SIR! HUMAN LIFE IS INVALUABLE. THIS ISN'T THE RIGHT SOLUTION TO THE PROBLEM.

OK! WE WON'T KILL YOU. GUARDS! PUT THIS PEST IN THE PRISON.

I HAVE DIPLOMATIC IMMUNITY.
WHAT'S THAT?

CHACHAJI HAS BEEN INSIDE FOR QUITE A LONG TIME. I CAN SENSE DANGER.

HEY! STOP THERE!

GET AWAY, YOU MOSQUITOES!

HOW DID YOU ENTER?
KILL HIM.

EVERY DICTATOR IS A BIT FOOLISH. THIS PRISON'S CONSTRUCTION IS SUCH THAT A LEAN MAN LIKE ME CAN EASILY SQUEEZE OUT THROUGH IT.

MY TURBAN !!

HEY ! STOP THERE !

THUDDDDD !
OUCH !!
www.chachachaudhary.com

6

SHOOOOT !
KILL HIM !

HOW'S THE RIGHT ONE?
THUDDD
OHHH H !

RUN !

YOUR EXCELLENCY ! HE'S LOCKED INSIDE !
GOOD ! BLAST THE BUILDING WITH A BOMB.
© PRAN'S FEATURES

7

NOOOO !
HOW DID THIS COCKROACH ESCAPE FROM THERE?

GUARDS ! SHOOT HIM.

HOW DARE YOU ?

WHEN SABU GETS ANGRY, A VOLCANO ERUPTS SOMEWHERE.

CRACKKKKK!!!
STOP HIM !

THIS PILLAR WILL SURELY CRUSH HIS BONES.

THUDDD!

AAAHHHHH! GRRRR!

LEAVE ME! I'M CHOKING !

COMMON PEOPLE.
KILL !!
KILL !!
KILL !!

HAVE MERCY ! I'LL QUIT FROM MY POST !
HAND DICTATOR ROTANDA TO THE PEOPLE. HE'S GUILTY OF KILLING LAKHS OF PEOPLE.

WE EXPECT THAT EVERYTHING WILL HAPPEN ACCORDING TO THE LAWS OF THE NATION.
WE PROMISE.
www.chachachaudhary.com

SPARK
DHAMAKA SINGH ! SEE, WHOM I HAVE BROUGHT ? WAR VETERAN JAXY.
IN THE VIETNAM WAR HE RUINED 15 TANKS AND IN THE IRAQ WAR HE DESTROYED THE ENTIRE COMPANY. NOW HE IS HERE TO HELP YOU.

BUT MY ENEMY CHACHA CHAUDHARY AND HIS COMPANION SABU ARE MIGHTIER THAN AN ENTIRE BRIGADE.

APART FROM THIS, WHEN THEY STEP OUT, THEY RIDE THEIR TRUCK DAGDAG.
WE HAVE A SOLUTION FOR THAT AS WELL.

THUMKA SINGH ! COME.
DHAMAKA SINGH.

I HAVE BURIED A LAND MINE HERE.

THAT TANK IS COMING. WHEN IT WILL CROSS THE LANDMINE, JUST WAIT AND WATCH THAT…
OIL CO
© PRAN'S FEATURES

BOO OM M M M!

JUST LIKE THIS, WE'LL DESTROY CHACHA'S TRUCK.
WOW !

NOW WE'LL PUT THE LANDMINE SOMEWHERE ELSE.
BUSU ! GO AND PROVOKE OUR ENEMIES TO PASS FROM HERE.

CHACHAJI ! SOME ROGUES ARE THROWING AN OLD WOMAN OUT OF HER HOUSE.
THIS IS INJUSTICE.
www.chachachaudhary.com

13

SABU! WE HAVE TO SAVE THAT HELPLESS WOMAN.

SIR! THEY ARE COMING.
GOOD!

HELLO! YOU PROMISED TO MEET ME TODAY.
DEAR! I'M STUCK UP IN SOMETHING IMPORTANT. I'LL BE LATE.

WHOSE PHONE WAS IT?
MY GIRLFRIEND CHINGARI. SHE'S VERY LIVELY. I LOVE HER VERY MUCH. WE'RE ABOUT TO GET MARRIED.

I CAN'T STAY AWAY FROM HIM. WHY DON'T I GO TO HIM?

OH THAT TRUCK DRIVER! HE'S NOT LETTING ME OVERTAKE.
HORN! HORN!!

WANT TO HAVE A RACE?
MADAM!! I DON'T COMPETE WITH FEMALES.
COWARD!

HURRAH! I OVERTOOK!
ZOOMMM!

SEE IS ANY TRUCK COMING ?
A CAR IS COMING AT A GREAT SPEED.

OHH! SHE'S MY GIRLFRIEND - CHINGARI STOP

LATE IN APPLYING BREAKS.
BANG! SMA SH!!

MADAM! YOU'RE BLOCKING OUR WAY.

FACEBOOK

DEAR! WHAT ARE YOU WATCHING ON INTERNET?
I HAD MADE MY ACCOUNT ON FACEBOOK.
CHECKING THAT ONLY.

WHAT'S THE RESPONSE?
26 LAKH PEOPLE HAVE BECOME MY FRIENDS.

WOW! ARE THERE FEMALES ALSO IN THAT?

YES, 45%...

TELL THEM, YOU HAVE A BEAUTIFUL WIFE WHOM YOU LOVE VERY MUCH.
OK.

MY LIE CAUSED THE COMPUTER TO BURN.

NO, JEALOUSY OF LAKHS OF WOMEN CAUSED THAT.

I CAN'T DEFEAT YOU IN TALKING.

WAIT! WHERE ARE YOU TAKING MY DAGDAG?
NOW IT'S MINE.

AND I AM ESCAPING ALONGWITH IT.

THE DOORS OF DAGDAG GET LOCKED AUTOMATICALLY, WHEN A STRANGER SITS INSIDE.

NOW YOU'VE BEEN TRAPPED.
© PRAN'S FEATURES

I'LL STARVE TO DEATH HERE...

HAVE MERCY! PLEASE FORGIVE ME.

OK.
WHISTLE

THE DOORS OPEN AT THE SOUND OF MY WHISTLE.

BYE !
www.chachachaudhary.com

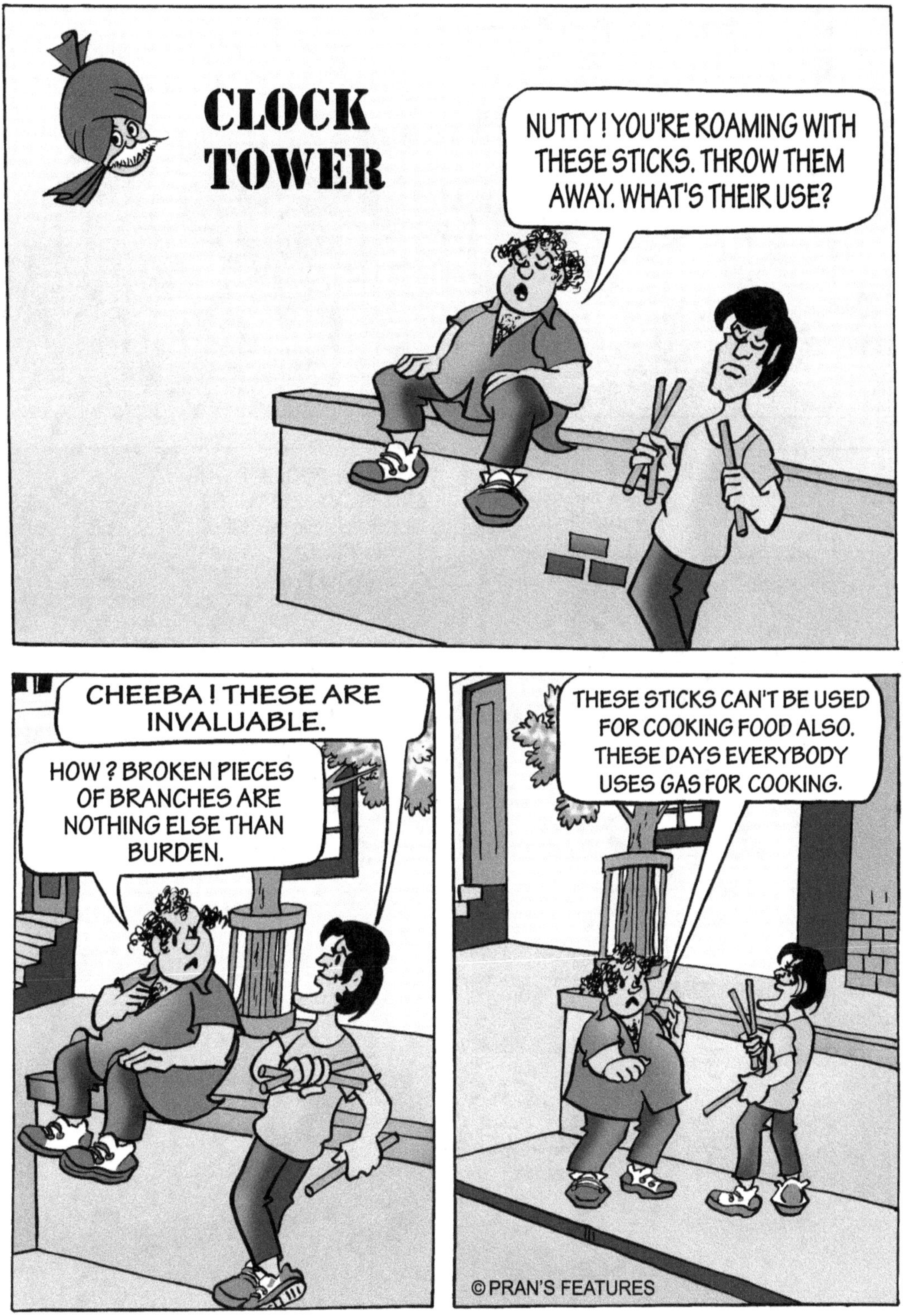

CLOCK TOWER

21

BUT, CAN'T THEY BE USED AS WICKETS?

BUT, STUPID NUTTY, WE DON'T PLAY CRICKET.

BUT ISN'T THE ENTIRE COUNTRY IS CRAZY FOR THIS GAME?

WE CAN BEFOOL ANYONE AND EXCHANGE THESE STICKS FOR SOMETHING EXPENSIVE.
I THINK I CAN UNDERSTAND YOU.

SEE ! THAT MAN IS WEARING AN EXPENSIVE WRIST WATCH.
I CAN SEE THAT.

SIR, ARE YOU FOND OF CRICKET?
WHY NOT?

DURING THE WORLD CUP I FORGET TO EAT, DRINK… AND REMAIN HOOKED ON TO THE TV.

THEN THESE HISTORICAL STUMPS ARE FOR YOU. THERE WAS A TIME WHEN THE FAMOUS PLAYER FAROOKH ENGINEER USED TO DO WICKET KEEPING WITH THEM.

PRICE ONLY 10 THOUSAND RUPEES.
BUT I DON'T HAVE THE MONEY.

NEVER MIND. WE'LL EXCHANGE THEM FOR YOUR WRIST WATCH.

BYE.

CHACHA CHAUDHARY ! WICKED NUTTY AND CHEEBA HAVE BEFOOLED YOU AND TAKEN AWAY YOUR EXPENSIVE WRIST WATCH. THESE STUMPS ARE THE STICKS GROWN IN MY GARDEN.

THAT WATCH WAS ALSO A TOY. BOTH ITS NEEDLES WERE STUCK AT ONE POINT.

BUT THESE STICKS?
IF NOT ME, THEY'LL BE OF HELP TO OTHERS.

SABU ! FIX THESE STICKS ON THE CLOCK TOWER.
SALE
© PRAN'S FEATURES

WOW !
NOW PEOPLE WILL KNOW WHEN IT IS 3 O' CLOCK.

MONEY MONEY

MR. KEY BOARD !
IS THERE
ANYTHING OF
MY INTEREST
IN THIS BOX?

MASTER SLATY KUMAR HAS WON
CRORES OF RUPEES IN INTERNET
LOTTERY. HE WILL OPEN A
CHARITABLE
HOSPITAL WITH
THAT.

HO ! HO !!
THAT ENTIRE
MONEY IS MINE.

SLATY KUMAR! DON AKA IS COMING TO TAKE AWAY THE MONEY.

COUNT AND KEEP IT READY.

MASTER KUMAR! I AM HAPPY THAT YOU'RE GETTING A HOSPITAL MADE OUT OF THE PRIZE MONEY.
HOW WILL IT BE MADE?

DON AKA IS COMING TO TAKE AWAY THAT MONEY.
HE CAN'T TAKE A SINGLE PENNY.
© PRAN'S FEATURES

LET'S GO TO THE MASTER'S HOUSE.
YES, BOSS!

RED TUBAN ! YOU HERE ?
CAME TO HELP YOU IN COUNTING THE MONEY.
www.chachachaudhary.com

THE ENTIRE MONEY IS KEPT IN THE TRUCK SO THAT YOU CAN TAKE IT COMFORTABLY.

FIRST I'LL HAVE A GLANCE.

COME, LET'S SEE.

OH !!
THUD !

NOW TAKE IT !
SHOOT !

HELP ME COME DOWN.

SWOOSH H !
GO !

SLATY KUMAR! START PREPARING FOR THE HOSPITAL'S FOUANDATION.

CHACHAJI! I'M GOING FOR A STROLL TO FRESHEN MYSELF UP.
I'LL GO HOME.

WHERE ARE YOU TAKING ROCKET?

THESE DAYS LOT OF THEFTS ARE HAPPENING. THIS DOG WILL GUARD MY HOUSE.

DO YOU KNOW THE DIET OF ROCKET ?

IF YOU TAKE CARE OF HIM, ONLY THEN WILL HE BE FAITHFUL.
OK. TELL.

ACTUALLY MY WIFE BINI TAKES CARE OF HIM. GO AND ASK HER.

OK.

MRS. CHAUDHARY ! ROCKET IS MY CAPTIVE. WHAT'S HIS DIET ?
YOU ?

A DOG CAN BE TIED, NOT A LIONESS.
www.chachachaudhary.com

SMUGGLER

CHACHAJI ! SOMEONE IS COMING TO MEET YOU.
THIS VEHICLE LOOKS LIKE THAT OF AIRPORT CUSTOMS.
CHAUDHARY SAHIB ! WE NEED YOUR HELP.
COME INSIDE ! WE'LL SIT AND TALK.

THE SMUGGLING OF COCAINE IS INCREASING. THE MINISTER HAS INSTRUCTED THAT IT SHOULD BE STOPPED.

ABSOLUTELY ! THE YOUTH IS GETTING RUINED DUE TO DRUGS.

DRUG SMUGGLERS ARE THE ENEMIES OF HUMANITY.

TOMORROW I'LL REACH THE AIRPORT.
THANKS !

NEXT DAY AT THE AIRPORT...
GREEN CHANNEL
RED CHANNE
www.chachachaudhary.com

GREEN CHANNEL
WAIT! A PLASTER ON YOUR RIGHT LEG?

MY BONE WAS FRACTURED IN A CAR ACCIDENT. THE DOCTOR PUT A PLASTER AFTER SETTING IT. SIMPLE!

I AM NOT A SURGEON. BUT I THINK MORE PLASTER IS APPLIED THAN NEEDED. LET ME REMOVE SOME OF IT. IT SHOULD MAKE YOU LIGHTER.

NO! IT WOULD HURT!

NOW THE PLASTER WILL BE REMOVED. CALL THE SECURITY GUARDS.

STAND
STRAIGHT.

PURE
COCAINE.

CHANNEL
RUN !

NO !

WHEN I SAW THAT HIS PLASTER IS UNUSUALLY BIG, I REALIZED THAT HE IS HIDING SOMETHING IN THERE.
CHACHA CHAUDHARY'S BRAIN WORKS FASTER THAN COMPUTER.

HAAKU

THIS SPACESHIP IS COMING TOWARDS THE EARTH FAST.

SPACESHIP LANDS DOWN...
www.chachachaudhary.com

THIS IS THE PLACE.

I'LL SET MY BODY ACCORDING TO THE EARTH'S TEMPERATURE.

AREN'T YOU CHACHA CHAUDHARY?
YOU ?

A REPRESENTATIVE OF EMPEROR HAAKU OF KARKETA PLANET.
SO ?

DICTATOR HAAKU LIKES YOUR COUNTRY.

HIS INSTRUCTION IS THAT YOU TELL YOUR GOVERNMENT TO ACCEPT TO BE OUR SLAVES.

AND PREPARE TO WELCOME KING HAAKU.
DO THE PEOPLE OF YOUR PLANET SEE DAYDREAMS ?

I HAVE COME AS THE MESSENGER OF PEACE... BUT YOU...

.... WILL HAVE TO BE DEALT WITH STRICTNESS. I AM GOING TO FINISH YOU.

ROCKET DOESN'T LIKE IT WHEN OTHERS BARK.
AHHH !
© PRAN'S FEATURES

MESSENGER OF PEACE! WANT TO VISIT A DOCTOR?
YOUR MEDICINE WON'T HAVE ANY EFFECT ON MY BLOOD.

HAAKU WILL TACKLE YOU.

COME, SABU!

INJURED THE MESSENGER OF HAAKU? HE'LL BE PUNISHED.

THE ANGRY DICTATOR MOVES TOWARDS THE EARTH.

THAT PEST WILL HAVE TO DIE.

WHEN SABU GETS ANGRY, A VOLCANO ERUPTS SOMEWHERE.

THUD D !
HERE ! TAKE THE RIGHT ONE.

LEAVE ME !

SWISH !
GO AWAY !

IT SEEMS WE CHOSE THE WRONG PLANET. LET'S GO.

THE CROW FLEW AWAY.

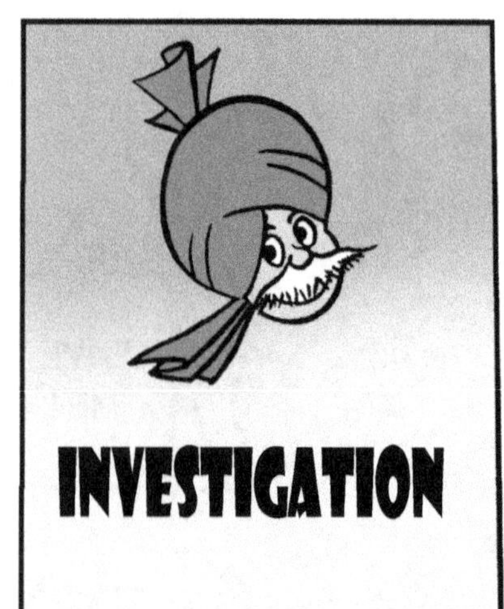

INVESTIGATION

LISTEN, JUST SEARCH ON THE INTERNET AND TELL THAT...

WHO'S THE OTHER MOST BEAUTIFUL WOMAN IN THE WORLD APART FROM ME?
THE SEARCH SAYS, IT WAS CLEOPATRA.

WHAT DID SHE DO TO RETAIN HER BEAUTY?
SHE USED TO BATHE WITH MILK.

NOW SHOULD I SEARCH THE ADDRESS OF MILK BOOTHS ALSO FOR YOU?
YOU MAKE FUN OF EVERYTHING I SAY.

SWISH...!
© PRAN'S FEATURES

OUTSIDE...
INSPECTOR MOZA ! HOW COME YOU'RE HERE TODAY ?
CHACHAJI ! JEWELLER HIRANAND'S SON RUBEL IS MISSING FOR 24 HRS.

I WANT YOUR HELP IN THIS CASE.
LET'S GO.

CAFE
WHAT DOES YOUR INVESTIGATION SAY?
POLICE
EVERYDAY RUBEL USED TO GET DOWN FROM THE SCHOOL BUS AND REACH HOME IN 12-15 MINS. BUT HE'S MISSING SINCE YESTERDAY.

YESTERDAY ALSO HE HAD GOT DOWN FROM THE BUS.

IT MEANS HE VANISHED FROM THE WAY AFTER THAT.
POLICE

HE WENT MISSING FROM HERE.
START THE INVESTIGATION FROM HERE.

WE ENQUIRE FROM THAT ICE CREAM VENDER.
ICE CREAM

DID YOU SEE ANY SCHOOL BOY GETTING KIDNAPED FROM HERE?
KIDNAP?
ICE CREAM

THAT CHILD USED TO GO FROM HERE EVERYDAY.
ICE CREAM
www.chachachaudhary.com

MAYBE HE STOPPED HERE FOR AN ICE CREAM. JUST RECALL YESTERDAY'S HAPPENINGS.
A CHILD HAS BEEN TAKING ICE CREAM FROM ME FOR 2-3 DAYS.

HE USED TO COME WITH A YOUNG MAN AND TAKE AN ORANGE ICECREAM…
MY FAVOURITE ORANGE BAR.

YESTERDAY ALSO THEY CAME STROLLING AND THE CHILD SAID…
SIR! TODAY I'LL TAKE A CHOCOBAR.
ICE CREAM

OK. TODAY BOTH OF US WILL HAVE CHOCOLATE ICECREAM.
THANK YOU, SIR!
ICE CREA

SIR ?
IT MEANS THE CHILD WAS WITH A TEACHER.

WE'LL HAVE TO GO TO RUBEL'S SCHOOL.
POLICE

PRINCIPAL MA'AM! PLEASE CALL ALL THE MALE TEACHERS OF YOUR SCHOOL.

WE HAVE ONLY FEMALE TEACHERS. NOT EVEN A SINGLE MALE.
?!

COME, MOZA! LET'S GO TO THE CHILD'S HOUSE.

THERE.
CHACHAJI! PLEASE SEARCH MY SON.
WE WILL FIND HIM SOON.

A YOUNG MAN COMES THERE.
ANY INFORMATION OF RUBEL?
NO, SIR.
SIR?

INSPECTOR! ARREST HIM.
TUTOR OF RUBEL. HE DAILY COMES TO ENQUIRE SINCE MY SON'S DISAPPEARANCE.

HE'S THE TEACHER WHO GOT ICE-CREAMS FOR RUBEL.

TELL, WHERE'S THE CHILD ? OTHERWISE I'LL CALL SABU TO BREAK YOUR BONES.
IN THE OLD CASTLE WITH MY UNCLE.

MOZA ! YOU TAKE HIM TO THE PRISON. WE'LL GET THE CHILD.

I'LL BREAK THE WALL AND ENTER.

WAIT ! LET ME LOOK THROUGH THE WINDOW FIRST AND ASSESS !
© PRAN'S FEATURES

I WANT TO GO TO MOM.
SILENT !

UNCLE ! YOUR NEPHEW IS REMEMBERING YOU.
CHAUDHARY, YOU?

WITHOUT THE RANSOM, THE KID WON'T GO FROM HERE.

YOU PUMPKIN !
THUD !

MY SON !
MOM-DAD !
GREED GIVES RISE TO CRIME.
www.chachachaudhary.com

48

CHACHA CHAUDHARY and PROFESSOR BAD

STROLLING IN THE FIELDS IS OVER NOW. SABU, LET'S GO BACK.
OK, CHACHAJI.

I WAS ABOUT TO SAY THIS AS I AM EXTREMELY HUNGRY.

REHTOO JI, TROUBLED?
ON THE WAY.

LET'S SEE, WHY?

WHAT'S THE MATTER?
I AM TIRED OF MY WIFE.

SHE WANTS TO DRIVE MY NEW CAR HERSELF TO GO FOR AN OUTING WITH HER FRIENDS.
GIVE THE CAR THEN, WHAT'S THE PROBLEM?

ALREADY SHE HAS DAMAGED MY TWO CARS BY HITTING THEM.

SHE WILL RUIN MY NEW CAR AS WELL.
YOU CAN EXPLAIN THIS TO HER.

ANY EXPLANATION WOULD OFFEND YOU.

OH ! IT'S A PROBLEM.

CHACHAJI, FIND AN APT SOLUTION TO IT.
I WILL HAVE TO FIND A SOLUTION.

OK !

I WILL JUST MEET YOUR WIFE AND COME.
© PRAN'S FEATURES

51

AFTER SOME TIME.
YOUR SMILE SAYS THAT YOU HAVE FOUND A SOLUTION.
YES. GIVE THE NEW CAR TO YOUR WIFE.

WHAT KIND OF A SOLUTION IS THIS? IF I DO THIS, SHE WILL DAMAGE MY CAR.

THAT WON'T HAPPEN.

TAKE IT.

BYE.

DON'T, WORRY YOUR CAR IS ABSOLUTELY SAFE. I'VE EXPLAINED YOUR WIFE.

WHAT DID YOU EXPLAIN TO HER?
I TOLD HER NOT TO HIT AN ACCIDENT.

IF SHE DOES SO THEN THE REPORTERS WOULD COME AND HER ACTUAL AGE WOULD BE DISCLOSED.

EVERY WOMAN IS SCARED TO REVEAL HER ACTUAL AGE.
GREAT! CHACHAJI YOU'RE A GENIUS.
www.chachachaudhary.com

THIS IS THE SECRET TO A HAPPY MARRIED LIFE.
CHACHAJI, SINCE YOU'VE MARRIED, HOW HAS BEEN YOUR MARRIED LIFE?

IT'S LIKE DRIVING A VEHICLE WITH ONE TYRE OF A SCOOTER AND THE OTHER OF A TRUCK.

SO YOUR CHACHI IS LIKE THE TRUCK'S TYRE, AND I, A SCOOTER TYRE.

CHACHAJI, IS THERE CO-OPERATION BETWEEN YOU AND CHACHI?
YOUR CHACHI AND I ALWAYS CO-OPERATE WITH EACH OTHER.

54

I MAKE TEA, SHE DRINKS IT.

SHE GIVES THE BAG, I BRING VEGETABLES FROM THE MARKET.

I CALL AND YOU HAVE FOOD.
OH! BINNY! I WAS JUST JOKING.

I AM WELL AWARE OF YOUR JOKES. LEAVE THEM. WASH YOUR HANDS AND MOUTH TO HAVE FOOD.

GOOD FOR NOTHING FELLOW !

ALWAYS READY TO EAT !

MY MOBILE IS RINGING, HERE COMES WORK.
TRIN TRIN !!

SMS FROM THE HOME MINISTRY, HAVE TO URGENTLY GO TO HOME MINISTER'S OFFICE.

WE HAVE TO GO. FINISH YOUR FOOD QUICKLY SABU.

YOU DON'T EVEN LET SABU EAT IN PEACE. HE HAS HARDLY EATEN 500 PURIS, 200 CHAPATIS AND TWO BUCKETS OF DAL!

EAT PEACEFULLY MY CHILD. I'LL BRING MORE FOR YOU.

IT'S YOUR LOVE THAT DOESN'T LET ME RETURN TO MY PLANET.
REMEMBER, SABU IS NOT FROM EARTH BUT FROM JUPITER.

VERY SOON.
WELCOME CHACHA CHAUDHARY !
THANKS MR. HOME MINISTER ! YOU CALLED ME ?

HE IS FAMOUS SCIENTIST PROFESSOR GOOD. HE IS DEVELOPING FUTURE READY CITY OUTSIDE THE MAIN CITY- IT IS AN EXAMPLE OF HIS TECHNICAL SKILL.

THIS IS WHERE THE PROBLEM STARTS FROM. PROFESSOR GOOD WILL TELL YOU ABOUT IT.

FUTURE CITY IS THE LATEST FUTURE READY CITY THAT WE'RE MAKING. IT'D BE CALLED THE BEST CITY OF THE WORLD. IT IS BEING TARGETTED BY NEGATIVE FORCES AT PRESENT.

ATTEMPT CAN BE MADE TO DESTROY THE FUTURE CITY. OUR DETECTIVE AGENCIES AND SPACE SATELLITES ALSO PROVE THE SAME.
MEANS ?

YOU'LL UNDERSTAND. SEE SOME OF THE IMAGES IN THIS TABLET.

THESE HAVE BEEN TAKEN FROM THE SATELLITES. SOME MYSTERIOUS RAYS HAVE BEEN SPOTTED AROUND FUTURE CITY. THESE RAYS ARE OF DIFFERENT SHAPES. WHAT ARE THESE RAYS AND WHY ARE THEY BEING SEEN AROUND FUTURE CITY— IT IS BEING SEARCHED.

...WE HOPE TO REACH A CONCLUSION SOON. BUT AT PRESENT, IT CAN BE SAID THAT.
www.chachachaudhary.com

FUTURE CITY IS IN DANGER, WE HAVE TO MAKE ALL ATTEMPTS TO SAVE IT.
YOU KNOW CHACHAJI, ANY SECURITY ARRANGEMENT IS COMPLETE ONLY WHEN YOU GET INVOLVED IN IT.

I UNDERSTAND.

YOU BE ASSURED THAT FUTURE CITY'S SECURITY IS MY RESPONSIBILITY.
THANKS, CHACHAJI!

YOU ARE ALWAYS WILLING TO WORK FOR THE COUNTRY'S WELFARE AND SECURITY. CHACHAJI, WHY DON'T YOU MAKE YOURSELF ALSO FUTURE READY? MY TECHNOLOGY AND I WILL HELP YOU IN THIS.
IT'S A NICE SUGGESTION, PROFESSOR GOOD! I WILL PONDER OVER THIS. RIGHT NOW, LET'S SEE…

.... FUTURE CITY.
WOW! WONDERFUL CITY!
VERY BEAUTIFUL! THAT IS WHY WE HAVE BEEN GIVEN THE RESPONSIBILITY OF ITS SECURITY.
© PRAN'S FEATURES

SECURITY ARRANGEMENT SEEMS TO BE WELL IN PLACE.

YES, THAT'S TRUE.

EVERYTHING IN ITS PLACE!
www.chachachaudhary.com

62

HAVE MERCY, GIVE ME SOMETHING!

SUCH A SOPHISTICATED MAN! WHO IS HE, CHACHAJI?
ISN'T IT A FUTURE MODERN CITY?

HE IS A MODERN BEGGAR, FUTURE READY BEGGAR!
BEGGAR?

HAVE MERCY, GIVE SOMETHING.
GO AWAY, I DON'T HAVE CHANGE.

IF YOU DON'T HAVE CHANGE, THEN A CREDIT OR DEBIT CARD WILL DO.

I HAVE SWAP MACHINE, I'LL SWAP IT.
WOW! BEGGAR HAS A SWAP MACHINE?

UNBELIEVABLE CHACHAJI!
NOTHING GREAT. HE'S A FUTURE READY BEGGAR.

IT'S MANDATORY FOR HIM TO HAVE THIS.

THERE SEEMS TO BE NO DANGER HERE.
NO DANGER COULD BE SEEN...

BUT THERE WAS DANGER.
FINALLY FUTURE CITY IS READY DUE TO PROFESSOR GOOD'S EFFORTS. BUT IT WAS MY IDEA, MY DREAM.

I WANTED TO MAKE IT MYSELF, FUTURE CITY. I WAS SEEKING PERMISSION FROM THE GOVERNMENT TO CONTROL THE CITY. IS IT WRONG TO BE THE UNCROWNED KING OF THE WORLD'S MOST EXCLUSIVE CITY?
© PRAN'S FEATURES

MY DEMANDS WERE GENUINE. BUT WHAT DID THE GOVERNMENT GIVE ME THE TITLE OF A TRAITOR, IMPRISONMENT AND DISRESPECT? THEY HANDED MY IDEA OF MAKING THIS CITY TO PROFESSOR GOOD. DUE TO HIS TECHNOLOGY FUTURE CITY IS STANDING FOR ALL TO SEE.

I WON'T LET IT STAND TALL FOR LONG !

I WILL RUIN IT !
WHAM !
WHAM !!

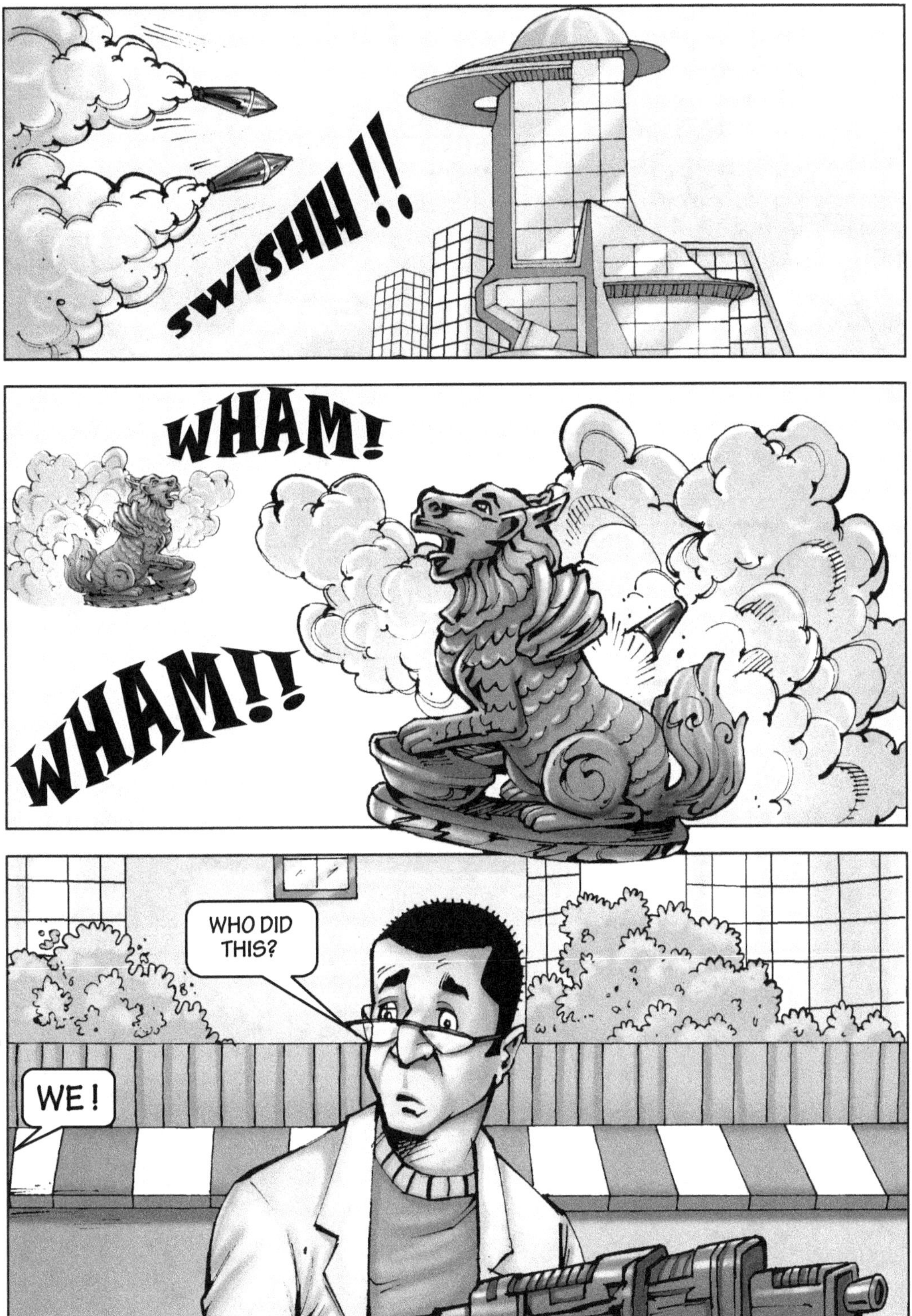

67

CHACHA CHAUDHARY ! SABU !

PROFESSOR BAD WILL RUIN THIS CITY. YOU WON'T STOP HIM.
SAVIOURS OF FUTURE CITY AND YOUR ENEMIES !

WHAM !
WHAM !!
YOU HAVE TO STOP .

WE KNOW HOW TO STOP YOU.
WHAM!
AND ALSO TO SETTLE YOUR BRAIN!
WHAM!
WHAM!!
ARREST HIM !

YOU WON'T ARREST ME.
OH !
OH !!
OH !!
YOU FOOLS ! DON'T COME NEAR ME.
I'LL TAKE CARE OF YOU !
WAIT, SABU !

THE CURRENT AROUND HIM CAN NOT ONLY HARM OTHER MEN BUT ALSO YOU.
FIRE !
HA-HA-HA- THE BULLETS CAN'T REACH ME.
THUD !!
THUD !
THUD !
HA-HA-HA !!

THIS SHIELD WILL SAVE ME.
MY SHIELD WILL ALSO ENABLE ME TO RUIN THE CITY.
WHAM
WHAM
CHACHAJI, PLEASE DO SOMETHING, OTHERWISE HE WILL POSE A THREAT FOR THE CITY.
WE CAN'T GO NEAR HIM DUE TO THE CURRENT AND ATTACKS FROM A DISTANCE WON'T AFFECT HIM AT ALL.
www.chachachaudhary.com

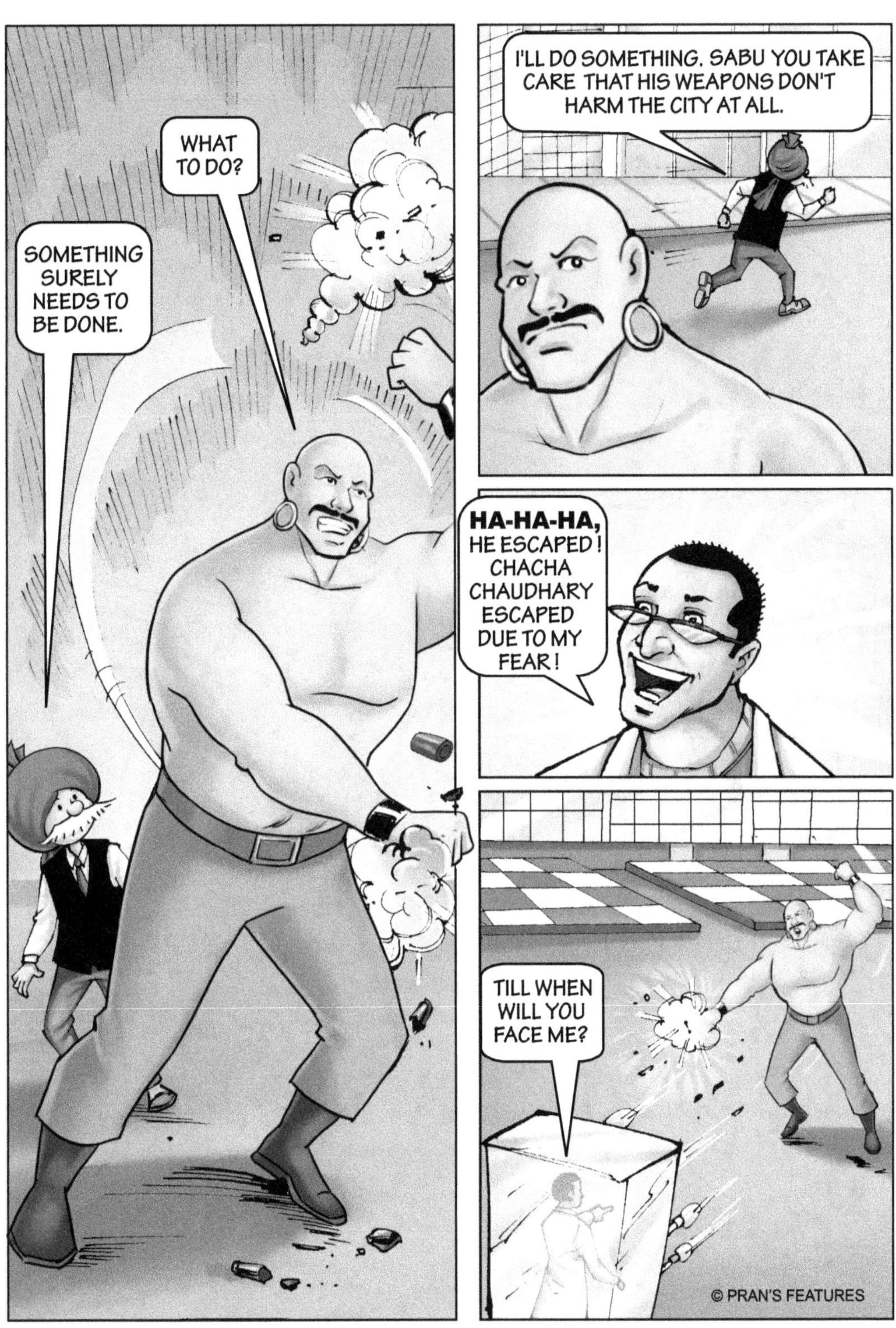

WHAT TO DO?
SOMETHING SURELY NEEDS TO BE DONE.
I'LL DO SOMETHING. SABU YOU TAKE CARE THAT HIS WEAPONS DON'T HARM THE CITY AT ALL.
HA-HA-HA, HE ESCAPED! CHACHA CHAUDHARY ESCAPED DUE TO MY FEAR!
TILL WHEN WILL YOU FACE ME?
© PRAN'S FEATURES

HOW CAN YOU SAVE THIS CITY FROM ME ?
OH ! HE'S RELEASING MANY WEAPONS AT THE SAME TIME. I'M AFRAID I MAY MISS OUT SOME WEAPONS SOON.
IF CHACHAJI DOESN'T DO SOMETHING QUICKLY, IT MAY POSE A PROBLEM.
I DON'T NEED TO DO SOMETHING, BUT A LOT MANY THINGS.
THAT TOO SOON !

IF I AM RIGHT THEN THIS SHOULD BE THE PLACE...

WHERE I CAN DO SOMETHING TO SAVE THE CITY FROM PROFESSOR BAD'S TERROR.

GHRRR !!

IT'S DONE !

HERE COMES PROFESSOR BAD.

WELCOME, PROFESSOR BAD ! YOU'RE WELCOME IN CHACHA CHAUDHARY'S WORLD OF PUNCHES.

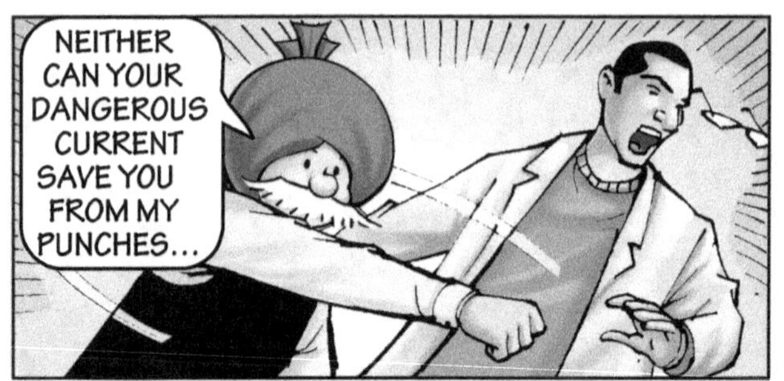

NEITHER CAN YOUR DANGEROUS CURRENT SAVE YOU FROM MY PUNCHES...

NOR CAN YOUR INVINCIBLE SHIELD!
WHAM!

COME WRESTLE WITH ME IN THIS DROWSY GROUND!

YOU ARE GREAT, CHACHA CHAUDHARY!
NOW ARREST HIM WITHOUT ANY FEAR!

HOW DID YOU WORK THIS OUT?
WHEN I SAW THAT NOBODY CAN REACH HIM DUE TO THE CURRENT AND THE SHIELD, MY MIND STARTED WORKING FAST.

THEN CAME THE IDEA.
HE WAS STANDING IN A ZONE OF THE DANGEROUS CURRENT AND INVINCIBLE SHIELD. BELOW THAT WAS AN OLD SEWER LINE OF THE CITY.
CHACHA CHAUDHARY'S MIND RUNS FASTER THAN THE COMPUTER.

THAT SEWER WILL TAKE ME TO HIM.

I ARRANGED FOR A ROAD CUTTER. THEN I REACHED RIGHT UNDER PROFESSOR BAD. THE RESULT IS IN FRONT OF YOUR EYES.

TAKE HIM AWAY.

WHAT WAS THIS THAT STUNNED CHACHA CHAUDHARY AND SABU? READ THE NEXT PART OF THE STORY TO KNOW MORE...

TIT FOR TAT

SIR! SAY SOME EXPERIENCE OF ARMY?

ONCE I WAS GIVING TRAINING TO NEW RECRUITS.

I NOTICED THAT ONE OF THEM MIGHT BE AN EX-CRIMINAL.

I SAW, EVERY TIME THAT PARTICULAR SEPOY FIRED, HE CLEANED AND REMOVED HIS FINGER PRINTS FROM GUN. THAT CONFIRMED MY SUSPICION!

TRUE!
© PRAN'S FEATURES

CHAUDHARY! NOW IT IS YOUR TURN.

ONCE A DICTATOR ORDERED TO PRINT HIS PHOTO ON EVERY STAMP .

AFTER FEW DAYS SECRETARY BROUGHT AND SHOWED POSTAGE STAMPS TO DICTATOR. BUT HE COULD NOT FIND HIS PHOTO .

WHERE IS MY PHOTO ? DICTATOR ROARED .

SECRETARY TURNED STAMP AND SHOWED DICTATOR'S PHOTO PRINTED ON THE SIDE OF STAMP WHERE PEOPLE APPLY SPITTLE .

HA ! HA !!

LET ME LEAVE. BINI IS WAITING FOR ME !

CHACHAUDHARY AND NET
SHUSHI ! MAY I HAVE THE HONOUR TO GIVE YOU LIFT TO YOUR COLLEGE ?
BANK
IT HURTS ME TO SEE MY WOULD BE WIFE WALKING AND GIVE PAIN TO HER TENDER FEET .
© PRAN'S FEATURES

FAST FOOD
Coke
MY DAD IS MINISTER AND VERY RICH . YOU'LL ENJOY ALL COMFORTS OF WORLD AFTER MARRIAGE .

WHY MY LITTLE TONY IS SAD ?
DAD ! I WANT TO MARRY SHUSHI, AND SHE DOES NOT EVEN LOOK AT ME .

SON ! DUMP HER . I WANT TO ARRANGE YOUR MARRIAGE WITH THE DAUGHTER OF VILLAGE CHIEF, GULLACK . HE CONTROLS FORTY THOUSAND VOTES.

SUSHI !-- SHUSHI!!-- SHUSHI!!!

I SAY, WHOSOEVER GIRL MY SON SELECTS, FETCH HER TO HIM . OTHERWISE, I'LL GO ON FAST .
WWW.CHACHACHAUDHARY.COM
© PRAN'S FEATURES

82

KIDNAP THE GIRL !

TONY WILL RECOGNISE HER.
CAR LOANS
TV
SHOES

THERE SHE IS .

HELP !

BINI ! GIVE ME REMOTE CONTROL FOR SOME TIME. LET ME SEE A CHANNEL OF MY LIKING .
WISEMEN SAY, A HUSBAND'S REMOTE CONTROL SHOULD ALWAYS BE IN WIFE'S HAND . OTHERWISE HE WOULD BECOME WAYWARD .

OKAY ! KEEP THE REMOTE, BUT PLEASE SWITCH ON NEWS CHANNEL .

BREAKING NEWS A GIRL KIDNAPPED IN BROAD DAY LIGHT ! NO CLUE YET TO POLICE.

CHACHAJI ! WHERE SUDDENLY WE'RE HEADING TO ?
SABU ! NOW WE'LL HAVE TO FIND THE DISAPPERED GIRL.
OASIS
DIGITAL
SHOES
SALE
© PRAN'S FEATURES

84

AT CRIME SPOT...
IN HURRY THEY DROPPED BOOKS, WHICH PERHAPS BELONGED TO VICTIM.
BANK
SUITS 50%

GIRL'S NAME ' SHUSHI IS WRITTEN ON BOOK. A LETTER INSIDE BOOK IS ADDRESSED TO POLICE SUPRINTENDENT PRAYING FOR PROTECTION. THAT MEANS, GIRL FEARED DANGER.

ROCKET IS PICKING SMELL OF SHOES OF CRIMINALS.

HE WILL LEAD US TO THEM.
HAIR DRESSER
PHARMACY

WE WANT TO GO IN.
ONLY ONE IS ALLOWED.

WHERE IS THE GIRL ?
CHACHA CHAUDHARY ! YOU ARE ENTRAPPED .

OUTSIDE YOU COULD HAVE CREATED TROUBLE FOR US . NOW YOU'RE UNDER OUR CONTROL.

YOU'LL BE OUR GUEST TILL I WED SHUSHI.
www.chachachaudhary.com

I HAVE NEVER SHOOK HANDS WITH A ROUGE SON OF A MINISTER. TODAY, PLEASE FULFIL MY CHERISHED DESIRE.
YOU'RE EMITTING FOUL SMELL.

IT IS COMING FROM MY PERSPIRATION SOAKED SOCKS, WHICH BINI DID NOT WASH FOR DAYS.

SHAKE HANDS !
KEEP AWAY ! I AM ALERGIC TO THAT SMELL. ITCHING HAS STARTED ALL OVER MY BODY DUE TO THAT.

GUARDS ! STOP THE OLD MAN !

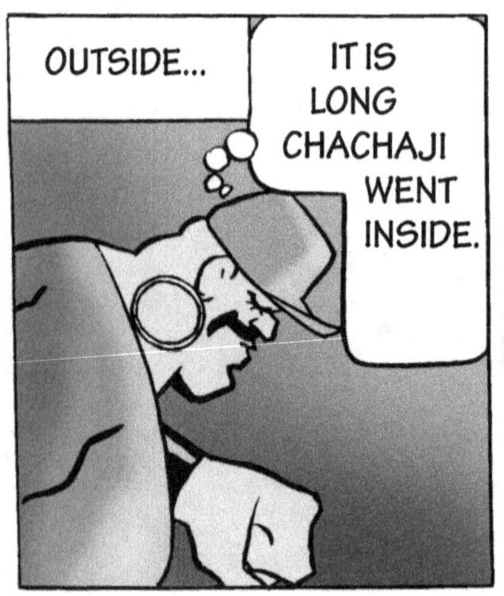

OUTSIDE...
IT IS LONG CHACHAJI WENT INSIDE.

FREEZE ! WE HAVE ORDERS TO SHOOT.
KILL !

RAT-TAT-TTTT !

THE MAGAZINE HAS EXHAUSTED.
TICK ! TICK !!

GET ASIDE, RODENTS !

BOOM M !
?!!

KILL THAT MONSTER !

AAWWW !
FIRST TASTE THIS !

WHAM M !
COCKROACH !
OOUWWW !

YOU ARE FREE.
THANKS, CHACHAJI.

RUN !
STOP !

DEAR MINISTER ! PEOPLE ELECT YOU SO THAT YOU SAFEGUARD THEM, NOT THAT YOU PUT THEM IN CONFINEMENT.
I APOLOGIZE .

CHACHAJI ! HOW DID YOU COME TO KNOW THAT FOUL SMELL OF SOCKS WOULD CAUSE ITCHING TO TONY ?
I SEARCHED FROM TONY'S FACEBOOK THAT MY MOBILE IS HAVING INTERNET .
CHACHA CHAUDHARY'S BRAIN WORKS FASTER THAN COMPUTER.
© PRAN'S FEATURES

FIND 2
THE SAME
PICTURES

Find the 10 differences